Copyright © 1995 by Nord-Süd Verlag AG, Gossau Zürich, Switzerland
First published in Switzerland under the title *Kleiner Dodo was spielst du?*
English translation copyright © 1995 by North-South Books Inc.
All rights reserved. No part of this book may be reproduced or utilized in any
form or by any means, electronic or mechanical, including photocopying,
recording, or any information storage and retrieval system,
without permission in writing from the publisher.

First published in the United States, Great Britain, Canada,
Australia, and New Zealand in 1995 by North-South Books,
an imprint of Nord-Süd Verlag AG, Gossau Zürich, Switzerland.
Distributed in the United States by North-South Books Inc., New York.

Library of Congress Cataloging-in-Publication Data is available.
A CIP catalogue record for this book is available from The British Library.
ISBN 1-55858-490-0 (TRADE BINDING)
1 3 5 7 9 TB 10 8 6 4 2
ISBN 1-55858-491-9 (LIBRARY BINDING)
1 3 5 7 9 LB 10 8 6 4 2
Printed in Belgium

Serena Romanelli

LITTLE BOBO

Hans de Beer

NORTH-SOUTH BOOKS

NEW YORK / LONDON

Bobo the little orangutan lived in the rain forest. Naturally, in the rain forest it rained a lot. And when it rained, Bobo was bored.

One boring rainy day while Bobo sat watching the raindrops bounce off his umbrella, he heard a loud rumbling noise. A large truck came rattling down the old jungle track. It bounced over a big bump, the back door flew open, and a box fell out.

Bobo hurried over to inspect the box. Inside he found straw, and paper, and finally another box—a kind of case, as black as a panther and shiny as a snake. Bobo shook it. There was something inside!

The thing inside was even shinier. Bobo sniffed it. He turned the case upside down, and the thing fell out, making a strange noise. Bobo leaped behind a bush. He watched the thing carefully, but it didn't move and it didn't make a sound. Bobo was a little bit frightened, but he was curious, too. Slowly he picked up a long stick that had also fallen out of the case. He tapped the stick against the thing. He poked at the strings, and *zing!* there was that strange sound again! Bobo was fascinated. He tickled the strings, delighted with the sound.

"What a great toy!" said Bobo. "Mother and Father will love it!"

Mother and Father did *not* love it. No one but Bobo did. He played with the thing all day and made such a racket that he gave his mother a headache. Finally, she stuck bananas in her ears to block out the noise. Bobo's brother and sister tried all kinds of ways to protect their ears, and the other animals stayed far away from Bobo and his noisy new toy.

One day Papa Tapir passed by. He stopped in front of Bobo and listened for a few moments. When he left, he was smiling, and the next day he returned with his whole family.

"What's going on?" asked Bobo's mother, and she took the bananas out of her ears to find out. What a surprise! She couldn't believe her ears! Bobo was making music—lovely, melodious music!

Soon the clearing in front of Bobo's home became a kind of theatre as more and more animals flocked to hear the little orangutan play. They clapped and cheered, and Mrs. Leopard even threw Bobo a flower after one performance.

How Bobo loved that music-maker! He was never without it.

One day, while swinging from tree to tree, a branch broke. Bobo managed to grab on to a vine, but his wonderful new toy fell *splash!* right into the river! Before Bobo could scramble down to the riverbank, a huge mouth opened and crunched the music-maker.

"Ugh!" growled Arnold the crocodile. "This tastes terrible! But at least there will be some peace and quiet again!"

Bobo saw pieces of shiny wood drifting downstream. That was all he saw, for his eyes filled with tears.

Days passed and Bobo grew sadder and sadder. He sat silent and forlorn, refusing to play with the other animals. His parents tried to cheer him with delicious fruits, but he wouldn't eat a bite.

"We must do something," said Mother. "Maybe Uncle Darwin can help."

"Good idea," said Father. "I'll go to see him right away."

When Father returned, he had a big sack slung over his shoulders. Bobo was so excited. "Here's my music-maker!" he cried.

There were many strange and wonderful things in the sack, but none of them looked like Bobo's music-maker. Bobo watched his friends having fun with all the new things. He felt like crying.

"I'm sorry, Bobo," said Father. "This was all I could find."

"Are you sure you looked everywhere?" Bobo asked. "Maybe if I went back to Uncle Darwin's with you, I could find it."

So the next morning at the break of dawn, Bobo and his father set out together. They walked along the jungle floor, they swung from tree to tree. Bobo saw many new sights—strange flowers, majestic mountains. When they paddled across a river, Bobo was so intrigued by the way the water reflected everything that he almost forgot about his lost music-maker.

"Welcome back!" called Uncle Darwin as they approached. The old orangutan didn't look very friendly, so Bobo hid behind his father's back. "Didn't your boy like the musical instruments?"

Father nudged Bobo. "No, I mean, yes . . . but . . ." Bobo answered. Then, summoning all his courage, he approached Uncle Darwin. "I mean, they were very nice, but they weren't exactly what the crocodile ate."

Uncle Darwin frowned. "Well!" he said gruffly, and Bobo trembled. "Well!" Darwin repeated. "I'm sorry. I gave your father everything I could find that made a nice sound. But since you've come such a long way, you are welcome to look for yourself."

He pointed to a dark stairway. Bobo headed down the stairs into a dimly lit cave. When his eyes adjusted to the gloomy light, he found himself surrounded by mountains of mysterious objects.

Bobo was amazed. "Wow!" he said. "A whole world of—"

"A whole world indeed," said Uncle Darwin, who had followed Bobo to the cave. "I collected these things from all over the world. Now, tell me, what did your music-maker look like?"

Bobo tried to draw on the dusty floor, but his picture didn't look very much like his music-maker.

"Well, then, how did you play it? Did you shake it or beat it?"

"I just held it . . . and then I took this stick, and then . . ." Bobo pretended to play.

"A violin!" cried Uncle Darwin. "I think I once saw a man playing one, but it was long ago, in my youth, so I can't be sure. Anyway, let's start looking."

Uncle Darwin and Father searched through piles of furniture while Bobo climbed the highest stacks, mumbling, ". . . violin . . . violin . . ."

Suddenly, from the top of the tallest refrigerator, Bobo shouted, "Look! Look here!" Bobo had found a case, as black as a panther and shiny as a snake!

It took all three of them to move the case out of the corner. Carefully Father lifted the lid, and inside lay a huge violin!

"A bit big for you," said Uncle Darwin, grinning.

Bobo didn't answer. It took all his strength just to hold this violin upright. He frowned. Then suddenly he smiled. "I know why it's so big. It's a mother violin. And where there is a mother, there must be a child!"

Uncle Darwin laughed. "A mother violin? This cello a mother violin? You probably think violins make nests. Ha, ha, ha!"

Uncle Darwin laughed so hard, he banged into the refrigerator. The door flew open and knocked him into a big pile of things, which came tumbling down around him.

When the dust settled, Bobo shrieked with joy. "Here it is! I knew I was right!" And there, inside the refrigerator, was a wonderful new violin, and it was just the right size! Bobo immediately began to play, and Father and Uncle Darwin applauded loud and long.

Bobo thanked Uncle Darwin over and over. Then he and Father set off for home. He carried the violin carefully. He couldn't wait to get home with his prize.

As they neared home, they heard an incredible sound. There was Mother, up in a tree, her ears plugged with bananas. Papa Tapir and his son rushed past them.

"What's going on?" Father shouted.

"Oh, nothing special. They've just started again." The tapirs hurried away.

There in the clearing in front of Bobo's home, his brother and sister and friends were playing the instruments from Father's sack. The noise was dreadful, but they were having great fun.

The dreadful noise didn't last forever. Bobo and his friends soon learned how to make beautiful music together. They formed a band, and in the evenings, when it wasn't raining in the rain forest, they gathered in the clearing and played late into the night. All the animals came to hear them, and sometimes they even danced.

And some nights, when everyone had finally gone to sleep, little Bobo climbed high into the trees and played sweet serenades in the moonlight.